O Nature, and O soul of man!

Moby-Dick

CATSKILL EAGLE

HERMAN MELVILLE

PAINTINGS BY
THOMAS LOCKER

PHILOMEL BOOKS
NEW YORK

To Candace Christiansen

T. L.

The text for Catskill Eagle is from chapter ninety-six,
Try-works, of Herman Melville's *Moby-Dick*
and appears in this picture book in its entirety.
Copyright © 1991 by Thomas Locker, Inc. All rights reserved.
This book, or parts thereof, may not be reproduced in any form
without permission in writing from the publisher.
Philomel Books, a division of The Putnam & Grosset Book Group,
200 Madison Avenue, New York, NY 10016.
Printed in Hong Kong by South China Printing Company (1988) Ltd.
Book design by Nanette Stevenson and Dave Gatti. Lettering by Dave Gatti.
The text is set in Kennerley.

Library of Congress Cataloging-in-Publication Data
Melville, Herman, 1819-1891. Catskill eagle/by Herman Melville;
illustrations by Thomas Locker. p. cm.
Summary: Melville's classic story of an eagle
who dwells in the Catskill Mountains.
ISBN 0-399-21857-2
{1. Eagles—Fiction.} I. Locker, Thomas, 1937-   ill. II. Title.
PZ7.M5166Cat 1991 [Fic]—dc20 90-20568 CIP AC
First Impression

A few miles from my home in the Hudson River valley a deep gorge called Kaaterskill Clove cuts through the Catskill Mountains. A hundred years ago the clove became a gathering place for many American poets, painters and writers who came to search for nature. Together they watched the silent sunrise, listened to the roar of the waterfalls and soared with the eagles. Herman Melville was among the writers who visited the clove, and in chapter ninety-six of his epic *Moby-Dick* he wrote about the eagle of the Catskill Mountains. After reading his words, I went with my family one summer to live in the clove and in my mind I saw.

—*Thomas Locker*

And there is a Catskill eagle in some souls

that can alike dive down
into the blackest gorges,

and soar out of them again

and become invisible
in the sunny spaces.

And even if he for ever flies
within the gorge,

that gorge is in the mountains;

so that even in his lowest swoop

the mountain eagle is still higher

than the other birds upon the plain,

even though they soar.